Bad Deal

Susan J. Korman

SURVIVING SOUTHSIDE

Bad Deal

Susan J. Korman

darbycreek

MINNEAPOLIS

Darby Creek
A division of Lerner Publishing Group, Inc.
241 First Avenue North
Minneapolis, MN 55401 U.S.A.

Website address: www.lernerbooks.com

The images in this book are used with the permission of:
© Image Source/Getty Images, (main image) front cover;
© iStockphoto.com/Jill Fromer, (banner background) front cover and throughout interior; © iStockphoto.com/ Naphtalina, (brick wall background) front and back cover and throughout interior.

Library of Congress Cataloging-in-Publication Data

Korman, Susan.
        Bad deal / by Susan J. Korman.
            p.   cm. — (Surviving Southside)
        ISBN 978-0-7613-6152-7 (lib. bdg. : alk. paper)
        [1. Attention-deficit hyperactivity disorder—Fiction.
2. Drug dealers—Fiction. 3. High schools—Fiction.
4. Schools—Fiction.] I. Title.
PZ7.K83693Bad 2011
[Fic]—dc22   2010023823

Manufactured in the United States of America
1 – BP – 12/31/10

FOR CONNOR, JACK,
AND KATE
—S.K.

CHAPTER 1

George!"

I had just reached the sidewalk when my mother called my name. I turned around. "Yeah?"

She stood at the front door, holding out a hand toward me. "You forgot something." She held a tiny blue pill in her palm.

"Oh. Right." I went to get it. "Thanks."

"That's the third time this week," she said with a frown.

"Yeah, yeah, I know. I'll take it at school. Promise."

She sighed, suddenly looking tired and sad. Our dog, Bart, stood next to her, wagging his tail at me.

"Really, I'll take it, Mom," I promised. "I gotta go. Bye."

"Okay," she said. "Have a good day."

"Thanks, you too."

I shoved the pill in my pocket and raced down the street. At the corner, the bus was already pulling away from the curb. "Wait!" I yelled.

It was my lucky day. For once, the driver actually stopped and waited. I hopped onto the bus and then slid into an empty seat in the back. I was on my way to another day at Southside High School.

▬ ▬ ▬ ▬ ▬

The morning dragged. During lunch period, I jammed into the crowded cafeteria.

I stood in front of the hot lunch selections, contemplating the lesser of two evils—greasy fish nuggets or beef Stroganoff? I asked for the nuggets.

"Fish for the Fish-man," my friend Ben sang out.

My real name is George. But since my last name is Salmon, everybody calls me Fish.

The lunch lady slid a plateful of nuggets toward me.

"They aren't bad with ketchup," I told Ben.

"Lots of it, you mean," he said.

We grabbed chips and chocolate milks and headed for our usual table.

Our friend Amy was already there, with a bottled water and a sandwich. The three of us had met in middle school, when we were all on the track team. I was the only one still running cross-country, but we still hung out all the time.

"No!" I moaned when I saw a notebook open in front of Amy. "Don't tell me you're doing homework! It's lunchtime, Amy. We're supposed to take a break from our 'studies.'"

"It isn't homework, Fish. These are my ideas for the science fair." She looked up at me and wrinkled her nose, which had tons of pale freckles. "I hate the science fair."

"Why are you doing it then?"

"College."

Ugh, the c-word again, I thought. I reached for a ketchup packet and squeezed ketchup all over my nuggets.

Amy watched me, making another face. "Fish nuggets? They look disgusting."

Ben was eating them too. "They really aren't that bad. Want one?"

"No, thanks. I think I'll stick with my turkey sandwich," Amy said and went back to her science fair list. While Ben and I ate, she read us some of her ideas. "How about this?" she asked. "Testing different kinds of juices to see which ones have the most vitamin C?"

"Bor-ing!" I said.

"Yeah, but it's chemistry," Ben pointed out. "So Mr. Allen might like it. I heard that he's one of the judges this year."

"Or . . ." Amy looked down at her list again. "What about testing different locations around school to see where the most germs are?"

"That isn't boring," I said this time. "Just gross."

Amy laughed, but Ben was nodding. "Yeah, do that one," he said. "I bet the most germs are in the cafeteria."

"I'm thinking the bathrooms," I said. "Or the water fountains."

"You're right, Fish." Amy wrinkled her nose again. "I don't think I'd have the heart for that one."

Kwame Williams, who was sitting one table away, heard us talking about the science fair. "I have a great idea for a project," he called over. "I'm going to test soil samples. If the pH levels . . ."

Blah, blah, blah, blah, I thought. It was one thing to spend my lunch period listening to Amy, who was one of my best friends, talk about the science fair. But it was a different story with Kwame. He was a nice kid—just way too intense about school. He wanted to be a biology major in college, which he talked about all the time.

While Kwame went on about soil samples and pH levels, I looked around the cafeteria.

It was my lucky day. Ella Lopez was only two tables away. She was eating a sandwich and laughing at something that Zack Cross was saying.

Zack was her boyfriend, although I had thought they had broken up again. I couldn't stand him. Zack strutted around school as if he were king of the place.

I watched Ella lean in to tell him something. *Man, she's pretty*, I thought. Her dark hair was long and straight and shiny and—

"Fish . . . Yo, Fish!"

Suddenly I heard laughter.

"Fish!" Kwame shook his head and grinned. "You were spacing out! I was asking you about the science fair."

"What about it?" I asked him.

"What are you doing for your project?"

"Nothing."

"Nothing? Really?"

"Yeah, really."

"Fish, the slacker!" added a kid next to Kwame who barely knew me. Steve Jones. "Maybe ADHD boy doesn't do science projects. He can't focus!"

Pretty much everybody at Southside knew that I had ADHD, attention deficit/hyperactivity disorder. I didn't really care what anybody thought. I just hated taking the medicine for ADHD. I couldn't sleep when I took it, and it made me feel weird.

"Fish can so focus!" Amy told Steve and Kwame. "Have you ever seen him draw? He's an amazing artist."

"He's pretty focused when it comes to video games, too," Ben added.

Kwame leaned over and slapped me on the back. "We're just messing, Fish."

"Yeah, I know," I said, spearing another nugget with my plastic fork.

A few minutes later, Kwame and Steve got up to talk to some other kids.

"All Kwame ever talks about is college," I complained as soon as they were gone.

"It *is* junior year," said Amy. "It's kind of hard to ignore."

"I know. But this is crazy: SATs, community service, teacher recommendations . . ."

Ben shrugged. "It's really annoying. But it's what you have to do if you want to go to college."

"Unless you're a really good golfer who's probably going to get a scholarship!" Amy teased him. Ben was one of the best golfers on the school team.

"I still have to take the SATs and write a good essay and stuff like that," he reminded her.

"I'm not sure I want to go to college," I burst out.

"What?" Amy's eyes went wide.

"Seriously?" said Ben.

"Yeah. You know me—I don't like sitting in school all day. And my mom is so worried about money."

"But, Fish," Amy said. "You have to go. If you don't, what are you going to do after high school?"

"I don't know." I shrugged. "I'm just saying, maybe I won't go. Maybe I'll do something else."

Amy started in again. "What else would you—"

"Excuse me, Fish?" someone said.

We all glanced up. Ella stood near our table, looking a little embarrassed. "Sorry to interrupt. Just wondering, are you free this afternoon?"

"Uh . . ." I blinked in surprise. In my three years at Southside High School, Ella Lopez had spoken to me once, maybe twice. And suddenly here she was—at *my* lunch table, asking if I was free.

Finally, I managed to get out an answer. "Yeah, I'm free."

"Oh, good." She looked relieved. "Because Sports Night is coming up really fast. And Miss Watts, you know, the art teacher, said you had signed up. The art committee is meeting at my house after school today." She looked at Amy. "You'll be there too, right?" Amy nodded, and then Ella looked back at me. "Three thirty, okay?"

"Sure, okay." I nodded. "Whatever you say. I'll be there."

"Great." Ella gave me a quick smile. "Thanks. See you later."

Amy turned to me, her mouth open in astonishment. "You didn't tell us that you joined the art committee for Sports Night!"

"Uh . . . well . . ." My face felt hot. "I thought I told you. I didn't really want to do it. But Miss Watts said I should."

Amy grinned. "So maybe you *are* thinking about college applications!"

"Nope," I said, watching Ella slip by a few people on her way back to her table. "That's pretty much the last thing on my mind right now."

CHAPTER 2

After school, Ben gave Amy and me a ride to Ella's house. Ella lived near him in a fancy neighborhood. My mother always called it "the other side of town."

Ella's house was as huge as all the other ones on her street. Out front, a landscaping guy was putting mulch around some tall trees.

I rang the doorbell, and Ella led us into the family room. Katie Lin and Jayson

Brown—the rest of the art committee—were already there.

"Whoa," I said, glancing at the wall over the fireplace. "Check out that TV!"

"Yeah, my dad bought it," said Ella. "It's huge, isn't it?" Then she got down to business. "So here's what we have to do for Sports Night. We need posters for the gym and the cafeteria."

While Ella was talking, I looked around at the rest of the room. There was a long brown leather couch and a glass coffee table piled high with magazines and books and other stuff. A gray cat was sound asleep on a chair. The walls were covered with pictures of Ella and her younger sister—at the beach, at Disney World, holding golf clubs, and playing the piano and the flute.

I felt really distracted, but I made myself tune back into what Ella was saying.

"We have to get all that done in about eight weeks. And we're supposed to stick to the theme—"

"What is the theme?" I blurted out. "Sports?"

Amy grinned at me. "Fish, the event is Sports Night. Of course the theme is sports!"

"Oh, right," I said, feeling stupid. "Well, maybe there's a special slogan or something."

"No special slogan." Ella was smiling at me too. "The theme is just sports. All different kinds."

"Got it," I said.

Jayson looked confused. "I don't really understand this whole Sports Night thing," he said. "I just signed up for the committee because Miss Watts told me it would be fun." Jayson was new this year at Southside.

"I can explain it," I jumped in.

"There are two teams with boys and girls mixed. Then there are a bunch of events— like relay races and gymnastics and dance competitions—that each team does to earn points. The team with the most points at the end of the night wins.

"It sounds dumb," I went on. "But it's fun. Lots of kids go to watch and hang out."

Jayson nodded. Then he and Katie and Amy said they would make the posters with all the details about ticket sales. That left Ella and me in charge of decorating the gym.

"We can put balloons and streamers all around," she said. "But we need stuff for the walls too." She showed me some posters that last year's art committee had hung up in the gym. They were mostly lame drawings of footballs and basketballs and goofy-looking dancers holding pom-poms.

I made a face.

"What's wrong?" Ella wanted to know.

"They're so boring. Do we have to make posters?"

"No. But what else is there?"

I thought for a second. "What about a mural? Wouldn't that be cool? We could make a really big one that wraps around the walls of the gym and shows athletes moving—like runners and gymnasts and dancers . . ."

"Okay . . ." Ella said slowly. I could tell that she wasn't sure about it, though.

"Here." I grabbed a few sheets of paper from the table and sketched a basketball player jumping into the air, about to make a shot. Next to him I drew a gymnast doing a handstand on a balance beam. Then I added a runner crossing the finish line. In my head I was picturing lots of different scenes. I drew as fast as I could to get my thoughts down on the paper.

"Okay," Ella spoke up suddenly. "I see what you mean now. Cool. Good idea, Fish." I looked at her, embarrassed. For a few minutes, I'd been drawing like a madman, totally forgetting about everyone else in the room.

My pill, I thought suddenly. *I never took my pill today.*

"But the gym is so big—a mural seems like a lot of work to me," Ella said. "I'm taking three AP classes, and the spring concert is coming up, and . . ."

"I can do most of the work," I offered.

"Fish draws really fast," Amy chimed in. "And I can help him. We can all work on it. We'll get it done in time."

Katie nodded. "It'll be fun."

I imitated the booming voice of the

athletic director at Southside, Mr. Gato: "Now that's what I call teamwork!"

Amy and Katie laughed loudly. I glanced at Ella, to see if she was laughing too. She was.

She's got a boyfriend, Fish, I reminded myself.

We decided to keep meeting at Ella's a few times a week until everything was done. Then we hung out for a while, just talking. When we went outside to wait for our rides home, I entertained everybody by doing crazy back flips across Ella's big front lawn.

Amy rolled her eyes. "Somebody did not take his medicine today."

"Yep," I said. "And that's definitely why I'm having so much fun right now!" I did a few more flips, making them all laugh.

Soon Katie, Jayson, and Amy left, and it was just Ella and me. We sat on a bench under some trees, waiting for my mom to pick me up.

"Thanks for all the help," she said.

"Sure." I shrugged. "I don't have much else going on these days."

"Really?" She looked at me in surprise. "Wow. I'm so busy all the time. After dinner, I have to put in some community-service hours at the hospital. And I have so much homework!"

"I have a lot of homework too," I said. "But I don't do a lot of other stuff. I just run cross-country in the fall and draw."

"My dad wants me to go to an Ivy League school," she said. "So I'm swamped with activities. Plus I have to keep my grades up."

I was trying to stay still next to her on the bench. But my legs were moving up and down like jackhammers.

Ella must have noticed. Because the next thing she asked was about my medicine.

"Doesn't medication for ADHD keep you awake at night?" she asked.

"Yeah, sometimes," I answered.

"That's what I need," she said. "Something to keep me awake, so I can study for physics tonight." She was smiling. But she looked sort of upset, too, like the physics stuff was worrying her.

I leaped up and reached into my pocket. "Here." I handed her the tiny blue pill. "It's my ADHD medicine. You can try it tonight."

She looked at the pill and then back at me with her big brown eyes. "Maybe . . . I do need to cram."

"Then take it," I told her just as my mother's old white car turned down the street. "Maybe it will help."

CHAPTER 3

The next morning, on my way out the door, I spotted my pill bottle sitting on the kitchen counter. I went over and started to twist off the cap. But something made me stop. I had slept really well last night . . . and Ella's had been fun yesterday too.

I put down the bottle. "Bye, Mom!" I yelled. I took off for the bus stop before she could come and make me take a pill.

School went fine. But back home later,

I was trying to study for the two tests I had the next day. And I was having trouble concentrating—lots of trouble. Finally, I got up and decided to take Bart out for a run.

I clipped on his leash and grabbed my iPod. Outside, I headed right to do our usual three loops through our neighborhood. My neighborhood looked nothing like where Ella lived. Here most of the houses, including mine, were small, one-story ranches with tiny yards. I was jogging past the Henrys' house when my phone vibrated.

I glanced at the screen. A grin spread across my face. It was a text message from Ella: Thanks for ur help with physics. I stayed up all night studying. Took test 2day. Ez!

ur welcome, I typed. Glad 2 help!

She replied a second later: Thanks again. See u 2morrow!

I couldn't think of anything to write back. So finally I just wrote something stupid: Sounds good.

Bart and I took off running again, this time flying past the houses on my street. *She's got a boyfriend*, I thought, reminding myself again. But at least we were becoming friends— maybe even good friends.

━━ ━━ ━━ ━━ ━━

When I got home, my mother was in the kitchen, making a salad.

"You're home from work early," I said.

She nodded. "Remember Dad's friend Bill?"

"Yeah?"

"I invited him to dinner. So you might want to take a shower," she added with a smile.

My dad had served in the Army National Guard, and his unit was sent to Afghanistan. Eight months later, he was dead. Since then, Mom and I kind of drifted through the days in separate orbits. We didn't talk much about Dad or how much we missed him.

After I showered, Mom asked me to set the table. "What are we having?" I asked.

"Steak, potatoes, and salad," she replied.

"'Kay," I murmured, heading into the

dining room with the dishes. I came back into the kitchen for napkins and silverware. "So why's Bill coming over?" I wanted to know.

She shrugged. "He came into Save-Mart last week when I was working. He asked how you were doing, and I thought it would be nice to have him over. He was one of Dad's best friends in high school, you know."

I still didn't get why she had invited him, but whatever.

"How's school going?" she asked as I counted out forks and knives.

"Good."

"Are you taking your medication?"

"What?" I spun toward her. "Why are you asking?"

"Well, because . . ." Her eyes flicked over to the bottle of pills sitting on the counter. "There are lots of pills left. And you're awfully jumpy."

"I'm mostly taking them. I just forgot a few times lately."

"George!" She frowned at me. "You have to take the pills! It's important—for school!"

"I know, Mom," I said. "But they m
feel weird. I'm never hungry and I car
Besides that, I . . ."

I let my words trail off. It was really hard
to explain. On the medication, I didn't feel
like myself. It slowed me down in a way that
I didn't like, and I felt spacey and strange,
like the real me was nearby, but floating
somewhere outside my body.

"We've been through this before, George.
The medication helps you pay attention."

"Nobody else has to deal with taking
medication every day," I complained.

"You aren't the only kid at Southside High
School who has ADHD," she said calmly. "I
know it stinks, but that's just the way it is.
Maybe by the time you're in college you won't
need the pills anymore."

"Maybe I don't need them *now*," I muttered.

"What?" She squinted at me. "What did
you just say?"

"Nothing. I'm just—"

Luckily, the doorbell rang, saving me from
having to say anything more.

"There's Bill," Mom said. "Please, just take your pills from now on, okay?"

"Yeah, okay," I said quickly. "I will."

I grabbed a bunch of napkins. As I headed back to the dining room with them, I spotted my mother taking a quick look at herself in the hallway mirror. "You look good, Mom," I said loudly. I meant to be nice, but there was a mean edge in my voice.

She flushed and then continued on her way to the door.

"Hello, Bill." I heard her say. "It's nice to see you."

━ ━ ━ ━ ━

That night, Mom and I did a good job putting on what my dad used to call the Salmon Show. With our guest there, we were funny and polite. We laughed at his jokes. We asked lots of questions about him and his family.

We found out that he had been divorced for twelve years. He was close to retiring from his job as a police detective. He had two daughters. One lived nearby, in a suburb of Houston. The other one had just moved to Oklahoma.

"So what do you plan to do after high school, George?" Bill asked me. We were carrying our dirty dishes into the kitchen. "Are you thinking about college?"

"Um . . ." As I put my plate on the counter, I noticed the bottle of pills still sitting there. For some reason, I didn't want Dad's friend to see it. "I think I'm going to college," I said, pushing the bottle behind some glasses. "But I can't stand talking about it."

"George!" My mother had come into the kitchen behind us. "Don't be rude."

But Bill just laughed. "You sounded like your dad just then."

I looked at him. "What do you mean?"

"In high school, your dad didn't know what he wanted to do either. But he got so tired of people asking him about it, he finally just joined the army after graduation. He said it was a way to get people off his back."

"Really?" This was news to me. But I didn't know much about my dad's career. All I knew was that he had been in the army for a few years. After that, he went to college at night to become an accountant. "I thought he always wanted to be an army guy," I said to Bill. "That was all he ever talked about. He seemed to like that a lot more than he liked being an accountant."

"Your dad enjoyed it, sure," Bill replied. "But it was never his big dream or anything."

"Oh."

A few minutes later, Bill and Mom poured coffee for themselves and took it to the living room. Mom asked me to load the dishwasher, so I stayed in the kitchen to clean up.

This probably sounds weird, but sometimes I still talked to my father. Inside my head, the two of us would have little conversations. That night, I checked in with Dad. I told him that I didn't know what to do with my life. Maybe I'd go to college. Or maybe I'd stay home and work. Maybe I'd even join the army.

"Don't worry, George," I heard him say. "You'll figure it out one of these days."

ChApTER 4

On Monday, Amy, Ben, and I stayed after school to watch a track meet. We knew a bunch of kids on the team, and it was a big meet against Uniondale—one of Southside's biggest rivals. Amy and I found seats in the bleachers while Ben waited at the concession stand.

Ella was sitting a few rows away with Zack and some other kids. When she saw me looking at her, she gave me a big smile and a thumbs-up.

I waved back.

Amy was watching. "What's up with you and Ella?" she asked.

"What do you mean?"

"Ella. The thumbs-up and the big smile. What was that about?"

"Nothing," I said.

"Nothing?" Amy repeated.

"Yep." Starving, I bit into the soft pretzel I had just bought.

Amy was still looking at me.

"Really. Ella and I are just getting to be friends. From the art committee."

"Okay . . ." she said slowly.

"She's nice," I added. "Don't you think so? And the art committee is fun. I'm glad that I told Miss Watts I'd do it."

Ben sat down on the other side of Amy. He was holding a hot dog with gobs of mustard. "Do what?" he asked.

"Art stuff for Sports Night," I said.

Ben started telling us about some events that he had signed up for. "I'm doing the golf relay. And one of the dance routines."

Amy laughed loudly. "*You're* in one of the dance routines?"

"Yep." He grinned. "I'm dancing with Lucy and Cate. It's going to be fun."

We watched a few of the track events. After the hurdles, I got bored, so I hopped up to buy a soda. Then I went over to bump fists with Ty Hendrickson, star running back on the football team, who was hanging out near the concession stand. Finally, I started wandering back toward the bleachers.

Suddenly Ella jumped right in front of me. "Fish Salmon! Just the man I want to see."

I grinned. "A lot of girls tell me that."

She laughed and tucked a strand of dark hair behind one ear. "Actually, I . . . uh . . . wanted to ask you about something." She lowered her voice. "I was wondering if . . ."

"I'm totally on top of Sports Night," I interrupted her. "Really. You don't have to worry about a thing with the mural. We have it covered."

"No, no. It isn't that." She stepped a little closer. "Remember that pill you gave me?"

I looked at her. "Yeah?"

"Do you think you can get me some more?"

"Oh . . ." I was surprised. "I think so . . . I mean . . . I'm not really taking them anymore."

"Are you sure?" she asked. "Because it isn't urgent or anything. But it worked great, and I just—"

"No, no, it's fine." I lied, rushing to reassure her. "The doctor said that I don't have to take them anymore. So honestly, it's fine. How many do you want?"

"Three, maybe?" Her face turned pink. "And . . . you know my boyfriend Zack, right?"

"Yep."

"He wondered if he could have a few, too."

My eyes flicked up to where Ella had been sitting in the bleachers. Zack was still there with some other kids. His dark hair was cut short, and he had a big, glittery diamond stud in each ear.

"You don't have to *give* them to us, Fish," Ella said quickly. "I mean, we'd *buy* them from you."

"Oh." I blinked, still thinking about it. The idea had never occurred to me before. I could feel Ella's eyes on my face. "Okay," I blurted out. "I'll sell some to you and Zack."

She smiled, and her whole face lit up. "Great. Thanks a lot. I'll text you, okay?"

CHAPTER 5

The next day, when we met to work on Sports Night, I gave Ella a few pills. But I wouldn't take any money from her.

"Okay, Fish," she said, giving in. "But when Zack gets in touch with you, you have to take money from him. Okay?"

"Yep. Sure." Zack had actually texted me twice already. But so far I had just ignored his messages.

On Thursday, I forced myself to sit down

to study for a test in U.S. government. I knew it would be a killer. Mr. Wood always made the tests hard. Not to mention the fact that I had done almost no homework lately. I flipped open my notebook and tried to memorize some of the important dates in Supreme Court history. But words and numbers kept jumbling together. And the reading was so boring.

Finally, I couldn't take it anymore. I got up and grabbed my laptop. Then I logged onto Facebook to see who else was online.

Ella!

Me: Hey. What's up?

Ella: Not much. Studying. Like always.

Me: I'm studying too. US gov test 2morrow.

Ella: UGH! U coming to the sports night meeting tomorrow?

Me: Yep.

Ella: Good. g2g see U 2morrow

No, don't go! I thought. I was trying to think of a way to get her to stay online when another message popped up on my screen.

This one was from Zack Cross: **Hey, Fish. Been trying 2 reach u. I'm looking for some**

extra help with school stuff. Can you meet me
2morrow?

I groaned.

Me: Yeah. Where?

Zack: Student parking lot before 1st period.
I drive a black Jeep.

Me: Got it.

Zack: Thanks. Later, man.

I logged off without bothering to reply.

━━ ━━ ━━ ━━ ━━

The next morning, I got off the bus and
headed for the student parking lot. Sure
enough, Zack was standing near his shiny
black Jeep, tapping something into his phone.

He looked up and saw me coming. "S'up,
Fish?"

"Not much." The pill bottle was in the
pocket of my hoodie. "So how many pills do
you want?"

"How many do you have?"

"I don't know." I took out the bottle and
looked at it quickly. "About fifteen."

"I'll take all of them," he said.

"All of them?" I couldn't believe it.

"Yeah." He laughed. "I have two AP classes this year. I can use all the study help I can get!"

I didn't know why, but I didn't want to sell all my pills to him. I didn't really want to sell *any* of my pills to him. But I had said I would and couldn't back out now. So I poured all the pills into his hand and then stuck the empty bottle back in my pocket.

"Thanks." Zack opened his car and dumped the pills somewhere. Then he handed me some folded-up bills. "Here you go."

I nodded my thanks.

"See you," Zack said. The bell rang, and he took off.

But I stood there for a second, counting the bills in my hand. I couldn't believe it. I had just made a ton of money—more than I had made working at All-Star Burgers for the entire summer. And it had taken me less than five minutes.

CHAPTER 6

Tap-tap-tap.

"Fish! Cut it out!" Brian Mosley hissed at me. "I can't think when you do that!" Brian sat ahead of me in U.S. government. It was the third time he had turned around to tell me to stop tapping my pen on the desk.

"Sorry," I mumbled.

I had finished the multiple-choice part of the test—mostly by guessing at the answers. But I still hadn't started the essays. Every time I tried to write something, I would start thinking about something else: what to have for lunch, Sports Night, buying a car . . . I already had about three hundred dollars in the bank. Now with the money I had just gotten from Zack, I could probably—

"What are you doing, Mr. Salmon?"

I looked up.

Mr. Wood had come up behind me and was standing at my desk. "The period ends in ten minutes," he went on. "And it looks to me like you're spending the time daydreaming instead of answering the essay questions."

"Yeah, yeah, I know." I started talking fast. "I'm planning what to write. I'm pretty sure I know the answers. I just can't figure out the best way to get it all down."

"I see," he said, giving me a look. "Well, keep your eyes on the clock."

I stared at the paper helplessly for a few minutes. Then I glanced back up at the clock. Seven minutes left. There was no way I could answer these essay questions in seven minutes.

I didn't know if I could even stay in my seat for that long.

— — — — —

"How was the government test?" Amy asked me at lunchtime. She had to take the same test later that day.

"Terrible."

She groaned. "Oh no. It was hard?"

"You'll probably do fine. But I had to guess at most of the answers. And the essays . . . I barely wrote anything at all."

"Last night, on Facebook, you said you were studying," said Ben.

"I studied a little. But don't worry," I told Amy, "you'll do fine. It's me. I couldn't concentrate."

Just then Amber Hynes dropped into the empty chair next to me. "Hi, Fish. Listen, I need a favor."

I looked at her, surprised.

Everybody knew Amber. She was one of the kids at Southside who liked to party.

But I didn't think she knew me—or even my name.

"I heard you're selling some stuff," she went on. "Can you get me a few pills?"

Across the lunch table, Amy's body went completely stiff.

I froze too, keeping my eyes on Amber.

"I'll get back to you, okay?" I said in a low voice. "What's your phone number?"

She gave it to me and I saved it in my phone.

"But you can get me some, right?" she asked.

I nodded, not knowing what else to do. I just wanted her to leave.

"Great," she said. "Thanks." Her silver bracelets clanked together as she got up. "Call me!"

"Okay," I murmured. "See you."

When Amber left, Amy was staring at me. "Oh my god, Fish. What was she talking about?"

I took a deep breath.

"Are you really selling your meds?" she asked.

"No." I shook my head. "I just gave a few to Ella. And then Zack Cross wanted some. So—"

"So you *are* selling them!" Amy finished. "I knew something was up. You've been acting weird lately—talking a lot more . . ."

I looked away.

"Why are you selling them? To make money?"

"I didn't mean to sell them." I tried to explain it to her again. "I stopped taking them, and then a few kids found out and wanted to buy some."

She shook her head. "That is so incredibly stupid. You do know that if you get caught, you'll probably get kicked out of school?"

"Come on, Amy," Ben said softly. "Chill. He isn't going to get kicked out of school."

"Well, he could! And this could ruin his chances of going to college, and—"

I slammed my milk container down on my lunch tray. "I am so sick of hearing about college! It's my life! Back off, okay?" Instead of waiting for her to answer, I stood up and dumped my lunch tray and then stalked out of the cafeteria.

CHAPTER 7

"George!" On Monday morning my mother
banged on my bedroom door. "It's late! You
missed the bus!"

I groaned and turned to look at my alarm
clock. I had spent most of the weekend at
Ella's, working on the Sports Night mural.
Last night, at around midnight, I had
realized that I hadn't done my homework. So
I had stayed up until two or three o'clock,
trying to get it all done. I had no clue if I

had forgotten to set my alarm or just slept through it.

"Come on." My mother pushed open the door. "You have to get up."

"I don't feel well," I mumbled. "My stomach hurts."

"Hmm . . ." She came over to get a better look at me and check my forehead. "You don't feel warm. But maybe you should stay at home."

She left for work, and I rolled over and went back to sleep.

At noon, I finally got up and went downstairs to make myself an egg sandwich. Then I played video games for a while. There wasn't much happening on Facebook, because everyone was still in school.

But Zack Cross had posted on my wall: **Thx for the study aids. U r the man!**

Amber Hynes had written something too: **Yo Fish. Any news 4 me?**

Oh, right, I thought. I had been so busy, I had forgotten all about Amber's request. I reached for my phone: **Sorry. All out right now.**

She texted me five minutes later: **u r going to get more right?**

I guess so, I thought. Sooner or later, my mom would have my prescription refilled.

Quickly, I did the math. If I sold another bottle of pills, I'd be a lot closer to buying a new car. No more school bus. No more borrowing my mother's car. I pictured driving over to Ella's in my own wheels. I just had to wait until I had more pills to sell.

Yeah. Will hook u up when I'm ready.

Cool. Thanks.

▬ ▬ ▬ ▬ ▬

In school the next day, Amy acted like nothing had happened between us last week and so did I. After school, Ben dropped me off at Ella's house so we could work some more on the mural.

Zack was on his way out the door. When he spotted me coming up the front walk, he grinned. "It's my man, Fish!" he said, shaking my hand. "How's the . . . uh . . . business?"

I looked away. "I wouldn't exactly call it a business."

"Right," Zack said. He still had a stupid grin on his face. "Because you aren't much of a businessman!"

"What do you mean?"

"I heard that you're all out of pills. You don't restock the store soon, you're going to lose all your customers!"

"Ha." I gave a short laugh. "See you, Zack." Then I pushed past him into Ella's house.

CHAPTER 8

Here you go, George." Miss Watts handed me paper and charcoal.

At lunchtime, I needed to make up some work that I had missed from when I was absent. There were a few other kids in the art room too. We were all working on still-life drawings that Miss Watts wanted to hang up for the art show.

I got started fast, sketching the bowl on the table up front. Then I drew the fruit sitting inside it. I was trying to capture the shadows around an apple when the phone on the wall rang.

Miss Watts picked it up. "Hello?" She listened for a second. "Okay, I'll send him down."

A second later, she hung up. "George, that was Mrs. Coleman. You were supposed to meet with her ten minutes ago."

"Oops," I blurted out. My guidance counselor. "I forgot about that."

"Well, she'd like to see you right now. You'll have to come back tomorrow, I guess."

"Sorry, Miss Watts." I put away my art stuff and headed to guidance.

When I got there, Mrs. Coleman did not look pleased with me. "You're fifteen minutes late, George."

"Sorry. I forgot," I mumbled.

She drummed her fingers on her desk. "This is important. You're more than halfway through your junior year. So you need to start planning for college." She nodded and then put on her reading glasses.

On the computer screen, I could see my transcript, showing all my high school grades. So far, my grades had been pretty good—mostly As and Bs, a few C-plusses here and there. I could also see that they had slipped a lot this marking period.

"You're still considering college, right?" she asked.

"I guess . . ."

"What schools are you interested in?"

"Um . . ." I tapped my foot and looked all around. Her office was messy, with lots of plants and thick books and binders. "I haven't really thought about it much."

"Do you know what you want to study?"

"Nope."

"George." She peered at me over the top of her glasses. "You were supposed to come to this meeting prepared. I asked you to bring a list of questions and a list of colleges that you might want to apply to."

I stayed quiet.

"What about art school? Have you thought about studying art somewhere?"

I shook my head. "I don't think my mom wants me to study art. She says it might be hard to get a job."

"Okay," Mrs. Coleman said. "So what else are you interested in?"

I just sat there. I didn't know what to say.

"Look, George," she said with a sigh. "I'm sure losing your dad has been hard on you. And lots of kids feel confused about their futures. But you have to start thinking seriously about this."

"I know." My eyes were everywhere but on her. I couldn't wait to get out of there.

"Going to college gives you more choices in life. So don't mess up your chance to go. Now let's figure out what you need to do to . . ."

She kept talking, blah, blah, blah, blah, but I zoned out.

I stared at the plants lined up on her windowsill. I listened to a jackhammer blast the sidewalk outside. I tried to remember the lyrics to a song I had downloaded last night. As I sat there, a few things she said, like *essays* and *SATs* and *community college*, slipped into my brain. But mostly her words just swirled around me like fog.

— — — — —

When I got home from school, my mother had the phone book out. She was frowning as she flipped through the pages.

"What's up, Mom?"

She barely looked up. "Car's at the mechanic. It broke down again."

"Oh, that sucks."

"We really can't afford a new car right now," she muttered.

"They'll figure out what the deal is. You'll get it fixed," I said, trying to reassure her.

She just sighed.

I went into the kitchen and poured myself a glass of lemonade. Just then my phone buzzed with another message from Amber:
Any news for me?

I stood at the sink for a minute, thinking. And hearing Zack's stupid comment again in my head: "You're not much of a businessman!"

He was right. If I didn't get more pills soon, Amber would buy them from someone else.

Back in the living room, my mother was still looking at the phone book and grumbling to herself.

"Mom?" I reached down to pet Bart. "Sorry, but I need to get a refill of my meds."

She looked up. "You do?"

"Yeah. My pills are all gone."

"Really?" She looked puzzled. "I just got them two weeks ago."

"I know. But I accidentally knocked over the bottle this morning, and the rest of the pills spilled down the drain."

"Okay," she said with a sigh. "I'll do that next. Right after I solve our car problem."

I went into my room and sent Amber a text message: **Back in business soon.**

Chapter 9

Mom got my prescription refilled. I sold a bunch of pills to Amber. Soon more kids were getting in touch with me to ask about buying my meds. One of them was Kwame Williams.

He waved to me in the parking lot one afternoon when I was waiting for Amy. She was going to drive us to Ella's.

"What's up, Fish?"

"Not much, Kwame."

"Hey . . ." He walked over to Amy's car. "I heard that you're selling your meds."

I nodded. "Yeah. I've sold a few pills. I'm not really taking them anymore."

"I don't know if I mentioned this to you, but I have a tough schedule this year. Do you think you could sell some pills to me and my friend? Like maybe a lot of them?"

"I have only a few left. And I'm not sure when I'll get more."

"Oh. Too bad." Kwame looked disappointed. "Do you know anybody else who sells them?"

I shook my head again. "Not really."

"Okay, well, thanks. I just thought you might know that doctor."

"Doctor?" I had no idea what he was talking about.

"I've heard there's this doctor guy who sells prescriptions or something. I'd contact him myself, but you know . . ."

Yeah, I do know, I felt like saying. Kwame was probably afraid he'd get caught—and mess up his "bright future" at some Ivy League school.

"Well, if something changes and you can get me some pills, let me know, okay?" he went on. "I'll pay you some serious bucks for them." He grinned at me and repeated it. "Serious bucks, Fish-man."

"Got it. Good to know."

We fist-bumped, and I watched Kwame walk over to his car, wishing again that I had my own wheels.

Some serious bucks, I couldn't help thinking, *would be a serious help.*

— — — — —

I was still thinking about my conversation with Kwame when I got off the bus the next morning. Amber was headed toward the school building too.

She pulled out the earbuds attached to her iPod and flashed me a smile. "Hi, Fish."

She's kind of pretty, I realized. Her hair was thick and curly, and her eyes were so light blue that they looked like glass. As usual, she had on a lot of silver earrings and bracelets.

"I'm having a party this weekend," she said.

"Yeah. I saw it on Facebook."

"My parents are going out," she said.

"Oh." I grinned. "Then it's going to be a really good party!"

"Yep. You should come. Bring whoever you want."

"Okay. Maybe I will," I told her. "Thanks."

As she turned toward her homeroom, I thought of something.

"Hey, Amber," I whispered, "do you know that doctor guy? The one who sells stuff?"

She looked at me closely. "You mean meds?"

"Yeah."

"I thought you already had pills, Fish."

"I sold most of them already. And now somebody wants more. And I need a car."

"Got it." She thought for a second. "You should talk to Matt—Matt Lee. I bet he knows that doctor guy."

I thanked her.

"Sure. Make sure you come to my party, Fish-man. Okay?"

"Okay." I nodded and then waved good-bye.

— — — — —

Matt Lee was a senior, so he wasn't in any of my classes. But Ben knew him pretty well because Matt was on the golf team. The next day, I heard on the announcements that there was a golf meeting, so I waited near the locker room.

Soon Matt came walking down the hallway, swinging his car keys from a lanyard.

"Hey, Matt." I hurried over. "I'm . . . a friend of Amber's. Fish? Maybe she mentioned me?"

He nodded.

"She said you might be able to help me out with something. That doctor who—"

He cut me off. "Keep it down, man."

I lowered my voice and told him what I wanted.

"I can probably get you a few pills," he said.

"No, no." I shook my head. "I don't want a few. I want a whole bottle."

"Ohhh." He nodded, getting it. "Yeah, I know somebody. You can have the prescription filled and then sell all the pills. I'll text you the information, okay?"

"Great." I gave him my cell-phone number.

That night, when I went into the kitchen for a snack, Mom was on a phone call. "Okay, thank you. I appreciate the call," she said before hanging up the phone.

"Who was that?"

She frowned at me. "Your guidance counselor. Sit down, George. You and I have a few things to discuss."

"I bet we do," I muttered under my breath. I dropped into a kitchen chair.

"First of all, you never told me about your college planning meeting," she started. "The one you almost missed—and didn't prepare for?"

I opened my mouth to speak, but she held up a hand, signaling for me to close it again.

"Second of all, your grades have slipped this marking period. Right now, you have several Cs, and maybe even a D in U.S. government. That isn't good enough. I don't know what's happening to you. But I don't like what I'm hearing."

We both let that sink in for a minute.

Then I spoke up. "I know. I haven't been very focused. I'll work harder. I promise."

"You had better work harder!" Mom said with a scowl.

I looked down at the floor and she softened your voice.

"You're so close, honey. Graduation is just one year away. If you can pull up your grades and then just stay on track, it'll be fine."

"I know."

She nodded and said a few more things to me. As soon as I could, I got out of there and went to check my phone again.

Finally, there was a message from Matt. He had sent me a name—Dr. Jim—along with a phone number.

CHAPTER 10

"How's the art for Sports Night coming?" Ben asked Amy and me.

It was Saturday night. The three of us had just seen a movie. Now we were hanging out at the Daily Grind, a coffee place near school.

"It's good," I told him. "We're making a mural for the gym."

"It was Fish's idea," Amy chimed in. "It's pretty cool. And let me tell you, doing art stuff for Sports Night is way more fun than working on the science fair."

"I still don't get why you're doing a science project," I said. "You complain about it all the time."

"I told you, Fish. It's for college." Amy's parents were both teachers. They were nice, but pretty pushy when it came to school stuff.

"It seems stupid to do it if you aren't really interested in science," I said. "But whatever."

Ben saw me looking at his giant chocolate-chip cookie and gave me a piece. "So how's Ella doing?"

"Okay." I shrugged. "She's still hanging out with Zack. They're at Amber's party tonight."

"Who *isn't* going to Amber's party?" said Amy.

Ben and I laughed. "Us!" we said at the same time.

Most kids from school were there tonight. But Amy had talked Ben and me out of going. We had decided that it would probably be too crazy with her parents not there.

yesterday, she had written on my Facebook wall again: Come to my party Fish! Or else!

Or else what? I thought now, even though it made no sense at all.

Mom came over and put an arm around me. "George, you're as white as a ghost. Are you okay?"

"Yeah, yeah, I'm fine."

"You weren't there, were you, George? You didn't go to that party, did you?"

I shook my head. "I went to the movies with Ben and Amy. Then we hung out at the Grind." I didn't tell her about Valeria stumbling in, drunk.

My arm felt numb as I lifted the phone in my hand to look at the screen—where there were sixty-one new messages.

CHAPTER 11

The next day at school was crazy with TV reporters and cameras. Lots of police, too.

In the morning, we had a schoolwide assembly. I looked around for Amy and Ben, and we found seats in the back of the auditorium. Mrs. Nuñez informed us that Amber Hynes had died over the weekend— probably from alcohol poisoning. And for the next forty-eight hours, the principal added, counselors would be available at school for anyone who needed to talk.

Next, one of the counselors walked to the microphone. "I know you've all heard this before, but we need to say it again: alcohol is a drug—a dangerous drug. Any time you take a drink . . . "

One good thing about having ADHD: you're used to tuning out stuff. I knew it was important stuff, so I tried to listen. I really did. But soon some other part of my mind just took over. And before long, I was tuning out almost everything going on around me: the crying kids, the blowing noses, the talking teachers, the buzzing cell phones—and the fact that I had been selling drugs to Amber. And whenever that thought crept closer, threatening to burn through the fog in my brain, I just made everything go blurry again.

— — — — —

I didn't go to Amber's wake or funeral. But a lot of kids did, and my mother made me send a card to her parents.

"It's the right thing to do, George. Even if you didn't know her very well," she said. "Remember how nice it was to get those notes from people when Dad died?"

I nodded and sent the card.

At school, things slowly went back to normal. But I still felt strange, like a robot or something.

There were only a few more weeks until Sports Night. On Saturday, Amy and I went to Ella's to work on the mural. Jayson and Katie were already there. We had finished sketching all the scenes. Now all we had to do was paint them.

Jayson, Ella, and Amy were working on a section with tennis players. Katie painted cheerleaders, while I worked on a football player catching a pass.

"So, you think kids will still go to Sports Night?" Katie asked quietly.

"What do you mean?" asked Jayson.

"Amber," she said. "After what happened with Amber, Sports Night seems . . . I don't know . . . stupid or something."

"I know what you mean." Ella looked up. "Amber won't be there. And everybody will be . . ." she swallowed hard, ". . . thinking about her. " She went back to painting.

"Did you guys go to her wake?" Katie asked softly.

The rest of us shook our heads no.

"It was awful. Kids were crying, and Amber's parents . . ." Katie shuddered. "They looked like zombies. I felt so bad for them."

"It's really sad," said Amy. "I can't believe she's dead."

"I know," added Jayson. "And it's so crazy about that other girl . . . Valeria? I heard she got in trouble for underage drinking and has to do community service."

"Yeah. I heard that too," said Ella. "Her parents totally freaked out."

For the rest of the afternoon we worked hard, adding more details to the mural. Amy left at four for some family thing, and then a while later Jayson and Katie had to go too. But I said I'd stay longer to keep on working.

Ella started painting a group of sports fans

in the bleachers while I painted grass for the football field. When I was finished, I went over to look at what she was doing.

For the crowd, we had drawn a bunch of anonymous faces. Kids our age with a few adults sprinkled in here and there. It was cool to see them come to life now, with color.

I looked closely at a sketch of a girl sitting in the middle of the group.

"What?" Ella was watching me nervously. "Did I do something wrong?"

"No, no. It's not that," I said slowly. "It's just . . . I have an idea." I picked up a paintbrush. Crouching down, I gently nudged Ella aside with my shoulder.

"Hey!" she cried, laughing as she tipped onto the floor. "This is my work area, Fish!"

"I just need a minute." I dipped my brush into the brown paint and added color to the girl's hair, making it look thick and curly. Next I painted her eyes—pale blue so they looked like glass. And finally I found some silver paint and added tiny earrings to her earlobes and bracelets—lots of them—to her wrist.

Ella was staring at the mural while I painted. "It's Amber," she whispered. "You're painting Amber Hynes!"

I nodded. "Now she'll be at Sports Night too."

"It looks a lot like her," Ella murmured. "It's cool, Fish—a little spooky, but cool."

"Thanks." I suddenly realized that Ella was sitting very close to me. When I turned toward her, I was staring right into her brown eyes.

"What are you looking at?" she asked.

"Your nose," I teased her. "Because there are . . ." Gently, I touched her nose with my finger. "A bunch of purple freckles on it."

"That's paint!" She laughed and kept her eyes locked on mine. "You're really nice, Fish," she said softly.

"So are you," I said. Then I leaned in to kiss her.

And she kissed me back.

CHApTER 12

I went to Ella's house a lot that week, working on the mural and just hanging out with her. Amy had noticed. "So, is anything going on between you and Ella?" she asked on Sunday afternoon.

We were at Ben's house, playing Xbox. I moved my tank across a deserted battlefield.

"Um . . . I'm not really sure."

And I wasn't sure about what was going on between Ella and me. We had kissed once more one day, but that was it.

"I think she likes you, Fish," Amy said.

I pumped a fist in the air and kept my eyes on the tank.

"That's cool," said Ben.

"Yeah, but . . ." I wasn't going to let myself get too excited yet. "She's still going out with Zack, even though she says she wants to break up with him. And she's really intense about school. So . . ." I shrugged. "Who knows?" Just then I spotted an enemy tank rolling toward me. I blasted it, creating a big fireball on the screen. "Gotcha!"

"My turn," said Ben. I handed over the controller.

Later, we headed out to Taco Shack for some food. In Ben's car, I got a new text message. It was Ella: **Bad week coming up Fish. Can u help me study again?**

Sure. I texted back. **Tomorrow?**

Sounds good. Thanks!

As we drove toward Taco Shack, I was thinking hard. After all the stuff with Amber, I had pretty much decided to skip my meeting with Dr. Jim. But I had only one or two pills left, and I really wanted to give them to Ella now. So what was I going to do when I was completely out? Ella, and probably Zack, would be asking me for more. And then there was Kwame . . .

━━ ━━ ━━ ━━ ━━

On Tuesday night, I asked Mom if I could borrow her car to go to a friend's to work on an English project.

"Yes, but . . ." She looked nervous. "Just make sure you have your phone in case it breaks down again."

"Okay."

I left, driving across town to Dr. Jim's office. On the way I flipped through the radio stations, trying not to think too much about what I was doing.

His office was in an old white house. I parked out front and then went around back to a rear entrance. A sign hung over the door: James Malloy, M.D.

Must not be a very good doctor, I thought, glancing around. Most doctors worked in nice offices. But this house looked run-down, with overgrown grass in the yard and black paint peeling from the shutters.

I pushed on the back door, but it was locked. I thought that was strange. I tried again, but the door still wouldn't budge. Then I knocked a few times, but no one came.

Next door, an old man was sitting in a lawn chair, watching me. He had on an Astros cap and was smoking a cigarette under a yellow light. "Nobody's there," he called.

"Oh," I said surprised. "I had an appointment with the doctor. Did he go out or something?"

To my surprise, the old guy let out a laugh. "Guess you could say that."

"Do you know when he'll be back?"

"Nope. No idea."

"Okay, thanks." I went back to the car and pulled out my cell phone. No new messages.

Maybe I'd gotten the time and day of our meeting wrong. I scrolled through my messages until I found the text from Dr. Jim:
Tuesday @ 9:15 pm

I had come on the right day and at the right time. So where was Dr. Jim?

━━ ━━ ━━ ━━ ━━

"Hi, George." Mom was drinking tea in front of the TV. "How did the English project go?"

"Pretty good," I said.

"Did you take your pill this morning?"

"Yep."

She smiled. "That's good."

I slumped on the couch and pulled out my cell phone again. I scrolled through my contacts and found Matt Lee's number. Maybe he'd know something about Dr. Jim. I sent him a message.

I half-listened as my mother chattered, telling me about how my father's friend Bill had come into Save-Mart again while she was working. They were doing inventory, and the customers were really annoying this time of year because . . .

I stayed like that, zoned out, until the ten o'clock news came on. That's when the announcer's words snapped me back to attention. "Our lead story tonight involves the shocking arrest of a local doctor who has been accused of illegally selling prescription drugs. A doctor residing . . ."

My heart skipped a beat.

I kept my eyes glued to the TV, where a dark-haired man wearing dark glasses—and handcuffs—was being led to a police car by two detectives. Underneath the doctor's picture was a caption that spelled out his name in big, bold letters: Dr. James Malloy.

CHApTER 13

I spent the next day freaking out. All I could think about was Dr. Jim and how he had been arrested. What if the police investigated his phone records? What if they found my phone number and my texts? Maybe they already knew that I was supposed to meet him Tuesday night.

In a panic, I deleted the two messages I had sent him from my phone. Then I deleted the one he had sent back to me.

At school, rumors were spreading like wildfire. A lot of kids were saying that Matt Lee—the senior who had given me Dr. Jim's name—had been arrested too. I had never heard back from Matt, so I had no idea what was going on with him.

I couldn't sleep. I couldn't eat. I couldn't think about school. All I could do was sit on the couch in front of the TV and stare into space.

Mom had noticed how jumpy I was.

"You're taking your pills, right?" she asked me on Thursday.

"Right!" I snapped at her, and she backed off. But the next night at dinner, she took a different tack.

"You aren't yourself, George. Is something wrong?"

"Nope." I bit into my burger.

"Are you sure?"

"Yep."

She was watching my face. "I heard you in your room late last night. Is the medicine keeping you awake again?"

"It *always* keeps me awake," I snapped. "That's why I hate it."

"Okay." She sighed and finally gave up. "But if something is wrong, I'm here. I'll help you. Remember what Dad used to say all the time: 'Every problem has a solution.'"

Yeah. *Except for this one*, I thought.

━━ ━━ ━━ ━━ ━━

After dinner, I went back to my room to do some reading for English. But I couldn't concentrate for more than five minutes. I got up and sent a few texts to Amy and Ben. Then I logged onto Facebook for a while. Finally, I headed to the kitchen to grab Bart's leash and take him for a walk.

It was a clear night. Bart and I jogged around the block. I didn't feel like going back inside and facing my mother again. So we headed in the opposite direction and jogged some more.

Bart was getting old, and he was panting like crazy. I stopped near a tall hedge to give him a rest. Above us, the stars were bright and the moon was full. I crouched down next to him, remembering how scared I had been of the full moon when I was a little kid. I had been terrified that it would turn me into a werewolf. So Dad would sit on my bed and tell me stories—funny stories to make me laugh.

I scratched Bart's neck under his collar. "I miss him, buddy, don't you?" The dog looked at me, still panting hard. Dog-speak for "I'm really thirsty. Can we please go home now?"

"Okay, Bart. Let's go, buddy."

When we reached the house, there was a dark car parked in our driveway. *That's weird*, I thought. I pushed open the front door.

"Oh, George! There you are!" My mother shot out of her seat.

Two men were sitting on the couch. One of them I recognized—he was my father's friend Bill. I had no idea who the other guy was.

"Hello." Slowly, I bent down to undo Bart's leash.

"Honey, Bill and Detective Frank want to talk to you about something."

"Policemen?" I froze, and the room began to spin around me.

Bill had stood up too. "Come on over and take a seat," he said, motioning to the couch. "We'd like to ask you a few questions."

My legs felt like Jell-O as I crossed the room and sat down on the couch. I sat as far from Bill as I could manage.

Detective Frank started talking. I heard a string of words. "Investigating . . . Amber Hynes . . . Southside . . . prescriptions . . ."

Soon I realized that Mom was talking to me. "George? Are you listening? Do you know anything about this?"

I turned toward her slowly, as if I were in a trance.

"I'll be blunt, George," said Bill. "We're concerned that you've been selling your ADHD medication to students at Southside."

"What?" A strange noise buzzed in my ears. "Really? What makes you think that?"

"We've been investigating James Malloy's phone records and Internet activity," Detective Frank said. He was huge, with a deep voice.

"And we've been monitoring Facebook postings by Southside kids. Your name has come up more than once."

"Well, that can't be," my mother blurted out. "George wouldn't do that. It's all rumors. Ever since Amber Hynes, the rumors have been just crazy."

I shook my head, forcing myself to look right at Detective Frank. "I'm not selling my pills."

"You're sure about that?" he asked.

"I'm sure," I said. But inside I was panicking. *Oh no . . . oh no . . . oh no . . .*

Detective Frank asked me another question. "Did you ever buy any drugs, or any prescriptions, from Dr. Malloy?"

"No." I shook my head, wondering if they already knew that I was supposed to meet Dr. Jim. "I mean, I know who he is from the news and everything. But I never met the guy. He sounds like a loser. A doctor? Selling drugs to high-school kids?" Suddenly I couldn't stop talking.

Detective Frank frowned and looked away.

Then Bill spoke up. "Well, I'm glad to hear that you aren't involved in any of this," he said, smiling at me. "As I'm sure you know, buying prescriptions from somebody—even a medical doctor—is illegal. And we wouldn't want you to get in trouble. Have you heard about Matt Lee?"

I blinked. So the rumors about Matt must have been true.

"Smart kid," Bill went on. "Hoping to go to Rice in the fall—and now . . ."

My mother stared at him. "And now what?" she asked.

"He has been charged with buying and selling prescriptions," the other cop said.

Bill looked back at me. "So if there's something you know, George, or something you think *we* should know, give us a call, okay?"

"Yeah, yeah, sure. Of course," I said. My voice floated over my head.

Bart had come over to lie at my feet. I sat there, petting him, while Bill wrote down his cell-phone number on a business card. He handed the card to my mother and then came back over to the couch.

He was smiling, and he spoke softly. But his words sliced through me like a sliver of glass. "Like I said, George, I'm glad to hear you're not selling your pills. Because this is an ongoing investigation. And sooner or later, we'll find out everything that's going on at Southside."

CHAPTER 14

"Every problem has a solution. Every problem has a solution." I kept hearing my father's words again and again in my head. I tried to tell myself that the words were true. That this problem—like all the others that I had had so far in my life—would work itself out. Then I could go back to living my life. My real life. The one where I wasn't scared all the time, waiting for Bill and Detective Frank to come and take me away.

Meanwhile, we had to get the mural done for Sports Night, which was coming up on Friday night. By Wednesday only one more section had to be painted—the last part, runners on a track. We had drawn a pack of them. But we had made sure to draw a Southside kid in the lead, almost at the finish line.

Since there wasn't enough room for everybody to paint together at once, I had offered to finish it.

Ella and Amy were hanging out, watching me. "Do you think you'll go to college for art?" Ella asked.

I flinched, making Amy laugh. "You're scaring him!" she told Ella. "Fish doesn't like that word!" Amy knew me really well. But this time she was wrong about my reaction. For once, it wasn't the c-word making me flinch. It was just any mention of my future. Which now seemed doomed.

"Well, you should study art," Ella went on. "You have talent. Maybe you could be a graphic designer or something."

"Thanks," I mumbled. "I'm not sure what I'm doing after high school."

Amy and Ella kept talking—about the science fair, about what Ella was wearing in her dance routine at Sports Night, about how much work AP Physics was.

I just kept working. I painted the group of runners, starting at the back of the pack and working my way forward toward the Southside kid in the lead. I filled in the colors of his uniform and then went to work on his face.

Jayson had been the one to sketch him. The runner was tall and lean, with long legs and arms. I painted his hair black, and then I made his skin dark.

When I was finished, I leaned back for a better look. *Perfect*, I thought. And I could tell from Amy's and Ella's faces that they thought so too. There was motion in his pumping arms and his striding legs and in the way the wind blew through his shirt. Even if you only looked at him—this lone runner—you could tell that he was it: the winner who would cross the finish line first.

Then suddenly I had a weird thought. Our runner would always be frozen there on the mural, racing like mad against the clock and the other runners, but going nowhere fast.

Just like you now, Fish, I thought, *moving fast all the time, but always stuck in the same spot.*

Everything that had happened over the past six weeks washed over me like a sudden tidal wave: hanging out with Ella . . . selling my pills . . . Amber's dying . . . the detectives at our house . . . lying to my mother . . .

"Woo-hoo!" Just then Amy let out a whoop, breaking into my thoughts. "We're finished, Fish! We're done!"

"Yeah! And it looks beautiful!" Ella chimed in.

I stared at them. I nodded and forced myself to smile. But suddenly I couldn't stay there anymore. "Do you guys mind if I go home?" I blurted out.

Amy was staring at me. "You look weird, Fish. Are you okay?"

"Yeah, yeah, I'm fine." I wanted to tell her what was wrong, tell her about all the bad things whirling through my head. But Ella was there, and I felt tongue-tied and strange . . .

"Sure, you should go if you have to, Fish," said Ella, cutting into my thoughts. "You did all the work tonight anyway."

Amy was still watching my face. But she didn't ask any more questions. She just nodded and said, "See you."

"Thanks. Bye," I said, and then I left.

— — — — —

"Can I talk to you, Mom?"

My mother was in the kitchen, unloading the dishwasher. She looked at me warily. Since the detectives had come to our house, the two of us had kept a distance from one another. She had asked me a few more questions about selling my pills. But I had just kept lying, insisting that I hadn't sold any of them.

"Sure," she said now, and we both sat down at the kitchen table.

I couldn't look at her. "I made a mistake," I began, "a bad, bad mistake."

She didn't say a word. She just sat there, waiting for me to continue.

So I did, telling her how I hated taking the ADHD medication and how I had wanted a car and how I had given away a pill and then I had sold some—and then I had sold some more.

Mom kept listening. When I was finally finished, she stood up and went over to the junk drawer. I saw her pull out a business card. "Come on," she said, grabbing her car keys. "Let's go."

My legs shook like crazy in the car. Mom's lips were white and pressed together. Neither of us said another word until after she had parked downtown.

Finally, when we were standing in front of a low brick building, she reached up to put an arm around me. In the sky, the moon was still full and very bright. I told myself that my father might be up there too . . . somewhere. Maybe he was even watching right now, waiting for me to check in with him again.

"It'll be okay, George," Mom said softly.

I nodded, hoping that she was right. Just then I felt my phone vibrate.

Amy, I thought, *calling to see why I had been acting so weird before*. I'd get back to her later—*if* I could—with a long story to tell.

"Let's go," I said to my mom.

Together, we walked into the police station.

About the Author

Susan Korman is the author of over thirty books for children and teenagers. She lives in Yardley, Pennsylvania, with her husband and children.

SOUTHSIDE HIGH

ARE YOU A SURVIVOR?

check out all the books in the

SURVIVING SOUTH SIDE

collection

Bad Deal

Fish hates having to take ADHD meds. They help him concentrate but also make him feel weird. So when a cute girl needs a boost to study for tests, Fish offers her one of his pills. Soon more kids want pills, and Fish likes the profits. To keep from running out, Fish finds a doctor who sells phony prescriptions. But suddenly the doctor is arrested. Fish realizes he needs to tell the truth. But will that cost him his friends?

Recruited

Kadeem is a star quarterback for Southside High. He is thrilled when college scouts seek him out. One recruiter even introduces him to a college cheerleader and gives him money to have a good time. But then officials start to investigate illegal recruiting. Will Kadeem decide to help their investigation, even though it means the end of the good times? What will it do to his chances of playing in college?

Benito Runs

Benito's father had been in Iraq for over a year. When he returns, Benito's family life is not the same. Dad suffers from PTSD—post-traumatic stress disorder—and yells constantly. Benito can't handle seeing his dad so crazy, so he decides to run away. Will Benny find a new life? Or will he learn how to deal with his dad—through good times and bad?

Plan B

Lucy has her life planned: she'll graduate and join her boyfriend at college in Austin. She'll become a Spanish teacher and of course they'll get married. So there's no reason to wait, right? They try to be careful, but Lucy gets pregnant. Lucy's plan is gone. How will she make the most difficult decision of her life?

Beaten

Keah's a cheerleader and Ty's a football star, so they seem like the perfect couple. But when they have their first fight, Ty is beginning to scare Keah with his anger. Then after losing a game, Ty goes ballistic and hits Keah repeatedly. Ty is arrested for assault, but Keah still secretly meets up with Ty. How can Keah be with someone she's afraid of? What's worse—flinching every time your boyfriend gets angry, or being alone?

Shattered Star

Cassie is the best singer at Southside and dreams of being famous. She skips school to try out for a national talent competition. But her hopes sink when she sees the line. Then a talent agent shows up, and Cassie is flattered to hear she has "the look" he wants. Soon she is lying and missing rehearsal to meet with him. And he's asking her for more each time. How far will Cassie go for her shot at fame?

THE PROTECTORS

Luke's life has never been "normal." How could it be, with his mother holding séances and his stepfather working as a mortician? But living in a funeral home never bothered Luke until the night of his mom's accident.

Sounds of screaming now shatter Luke's dreams. And his stepfather is acting even stranger. When bodies in the funeral home start delivering messages, Luke is certain that he's nuts. As he tries to solve his mother's death, Luke discovers a secret more horrifying than any nightmare.

SKIN

It looks like a pizza exploded on Nick Barry's face. But bad skin is the least of his problems. His bones feel like living ice. A strange rash—like scratches—seems to be some sort of ancient code. And then there's the anger . . .

Something evil is living under Nick's skin. Where did it come from? What does it want? With the help of a dead kid's diary, a nun, and a local professor, Nick slowly finds out what's wrong with him. But there's still one question that Nick must face alone: how do you destroy an evil that's *inside* you?

THAW

A July storm caused a major power outage in Bridgewater. Now a research project at the Institute for Cryogenic Experimentation has been ruined, and the thawed-out bodies of twenty-seven federal inmates are missing.

At first, Dani didn't think much of the news. But after her best friend Jake disappears, a mysterious visitor connects the dots for Dani. Jake has been taken in by a cult. To get him back, Dani must enter a dangerous, alternate reality where a defrosted cult leader is beginning to act like some kind of god.

UNTHINKABLE

Omar Phillips is Bridgewater High's favorite teen author. His fans can't wait for his next horror story. But lately Omar's imagination has turned against him. Horrifying visions of death and destruction haunt him. The only way to stop the visions is to write them down. Until they start coming true . . .

Enter Sophie Minax, the mysterious girl who's been following Omar at school. "I'm one of you," Sophie says. She tells Omar how to end the visions—but the only thing worse than Sophie's cure may be what happens if he ignores it.

THE CLUB

The club started innocently enough. Bored after school, Josh and his friends decided to try out an old board game. Called "Black Magic," it promised players good fortune at the expense of those who have wronged them.

But when the club members' luck starts skyrocketing—and horror befalls their enemies—the game stops being a joke. How can they stop what they've unleashed? Answers lie in an old diary—but ending the game may be deadlier than any curse.

MESSAGES FROM BEYOND

Some guy named Ethan has been texting Cassie. He seems to know all about her—but she can't place him. He's not in the yearbook either. Cassie thinks one of her friends is punking her. But she can't ignore the strange coincidences—like how Ethan looks just like the guy in her nightmares.

Cassie's search for Ethan leads her to a shocking discovery—and a struggle for her life. Will Cassie be able to break free from her mysterious stalker?